# KNIGHT OWLS

by Eric Seltzer
illustrated by Tom Disbury

Ready-to-Read

Simon Spotlight

New York    London    Toronto    Sydney    New Delhi

For Suzy Capozzi, with many thanks—E. S.

For Shiv—T. D.

SIMON SPOTLIGHT
An imprint of Simon & Schuster Children's Publishing Division
1230 Avenue of the Americas, New York, New York 10020
This Simon Spotlight edition September 2019
Text copyright © 2019 by Eric Seltzer
Illustrations copyright © 2019 by Tom Disbury
For information about special discounts for bulk purchases, please contact
Simon & Schuster Special Sales at 1-866-506-1949
or business@simonandschuster.com.
Manufactured in the United States of America 1121 LAK
6  8  10  9  7  5
Library of Congress Cataloging-in-Publication Data
Names: Seltzer, Eric, author. | Disbury, Tom, illustrator.
Title: Knight owls / by Eric Seltzer ; illustrated by Tom Disbury.
Description: New York : Simon Spotlight, 2019. | Series: Ready-to-read.
Prelevel 1 | Summary: Illustrations and easy-to-read, rhyming text follow a
band of knight owls as they demonstrate their strength, courage, and kindness,
even when facing Phil the dragon.
Identifiers: LCCN 2019014670 | ISBN 9781534448803 (paperback) |
ISBN 9781534448810 (hardcover) | ISBN 9781534448827 (eBook)
Subjects: | CYAC: Stories in rhyme. | Knights and knighthood—Fiction. |
Owls—Fiction. | Humorous stories. | BISAC: JUVENILE FICTION / Readers /
Beginner. | JUVENILE FICTION / Humorous Stories.
JUVENILE FICTION / Animals / Birds.
Classification: LCC PZ8.3.S4665 Kni 2019 | DDC [E]—dc23
LC record available at https://lccn.loc.gov/2019014670

# Knight owls are strong.

Knight owls
are brave.

# Knight owls are kind.

See this one wave.

Knight owls help
the king and the queen,

and all the owls
in between.

Some stay
up late.

Some love reading.

If there is time,
they do good-deeding.

# All knights
## need a dragon.

This one's name is Phil.

Last week, Phil
made a mess of the mill.

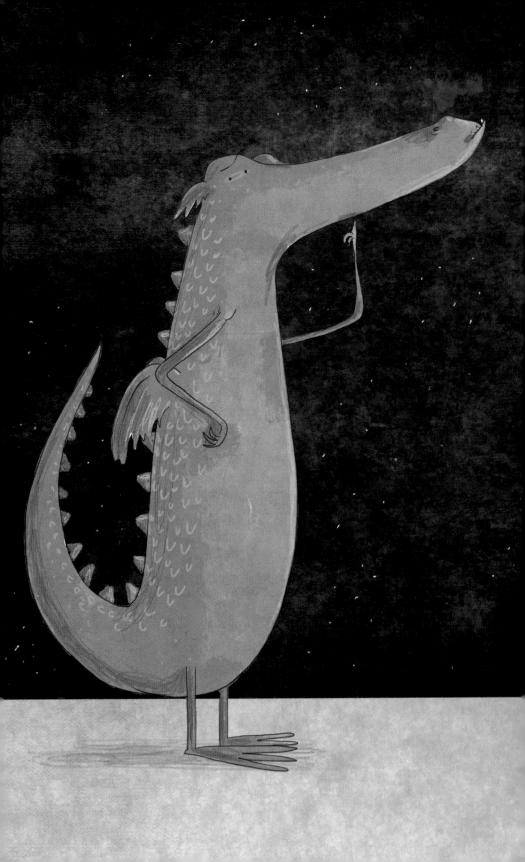

The owls warned Phil:
Use your head,
and do something good
instead.

So Phil baked pizza
with lots of cheese.

And sure enough,
it seemed to please.

The village is safe.

Phil is branching out.

He is learning what
friendship (and cooking)
is all about.

Now everyone is happy.

They all get along.

They even sing Phil
a happy song.